this
little
light
of
mine

illustrated by E. B. Lewis

Simon & Schuster Books for Young Readers
New York   London   Toronto   Sydney

This little light of mine,
I'm gonna let it shine.

This little light of mine,
I'm gonna let it shine.

This little light of mine,
I'm gonna let it shine.

Let it shine,
let it shine,
let it shine.

Hide it under a bushel? No!
I'm gonna let it shine.

Hide it under a bushel? No!
I'm gonna let it shine.

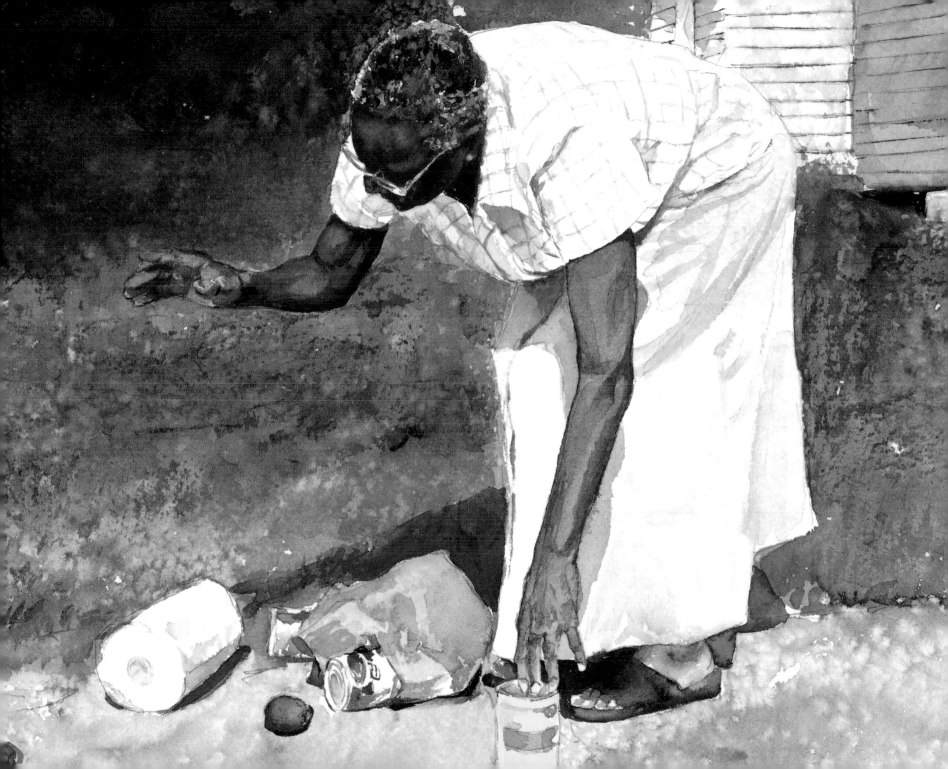

Hide it under a bushel? No!
I'm gonna let it shine.

Let it shine,
let it shine,
let it shine.

Won't let no one blow it out,
I'm gonna let it shine.

Won't let no one blow it out,
I'm gonna let it shine.

Won't let no one blow it out,
I'm gonna let it shine.

Let it shine,
let it shine,
let it shine.

Ev'rywhere I go,
I'm gonna let it shine.

Ev'rywhere I go,
I'm gonna let it shine.

Ev'rywhere I go,
I'm gonna let it shine.

Let it shine,
let it shine,
let it shine.

This Little Light of Mine

Arr. David M. Thomas

To my sons, Aaron and Josh, who are truly my light—E. B. Lewis

SIMON & SCHUSTER BOOKS FOR YOUNG READERS

An imprint of Simon & Schuster Children's Publishing Division

1230 Avenue of the Americas, New York, New York 10020

Illustrations copyright © 2005 by E. B. Lewis

SIMON & SCHUSTER BOOKS FOR YOUNG READERS is a trademark of Simon & Schuster, Inc.

Book design by Dan Potash

The text for this book is set in Vendome.

The illustrations for this book are rendered in watercolor.

Manufactured in China

2 4 6 8 10 9 7 5 3 1

CIP data for this book is available from the Library of Congress.

ISBN 0-689-83179-X

Score on page 31 adapted from *All Night, All Day: A Child's First Book of African-American Spirituals,* copyright © 1991 selected and illustrated by Ashley Bryan.